PALAMPAM DAY

by David and Phillis Gershator

illustrated by Enrique O. Sánchez

MARSHALL CAVENDISH   NEW YORK

Text copyright © 1997 by David and Phillis Gershator
Illustrations © 1997 by Enrique O. Sanchez
All rights reserved
Marshall Cavendish, 99 White Plains Road, Tarrytown, New York 10591
The text of this book is set in 14 point Panache Bold
The illustrations are acrylic gouache painting
Printed in Italy
First edition
1 3 5 6 4 2

Library of Congress Cataloging-in-Publication Data
Gershator, David.
Palampam Day / David and Phillis Gershator : illustrated by Enrique O. Sanchez.
p.   cm   Summary: One day when the coconuts, dogs, frogs, fish, and bananas talk to him,
Turo goes to ask wise old Papa Tata Wanga for advice.
ISBN 0-7614-5002-5 (reinf. bndg.)
(1. West Indies—Fiction.) I. Gershator, Phillis. II. Sanchez, Enrique O., date, 1997 ill. III. Title.
PZ7.G314PA1   (E)—dc21   96-54899 CIP AC

*To Judith Whipple, for the wisdom
of a Papa Tata Wanga*—D. G. & P. G.

For Misha—E. O. S.

One morning, Turo climbed a coconut palm down by Coconut Beach. Just as he reached out to pick a big, brown, ripe coconut, he heard a voice.

"Don't pick me, *mon!*"

Turo was astonished. "Did I hear a coconut talking?"

Another coconut spoke up. "Better do what Cousin Coconut said, before you fall and crack your head."

Turo slid down the tall coconut palm as fast as he could. He wasn't ready to talk to coconuts so early in the morning. And he wasn't ready to fall on his head, or break a leg either.

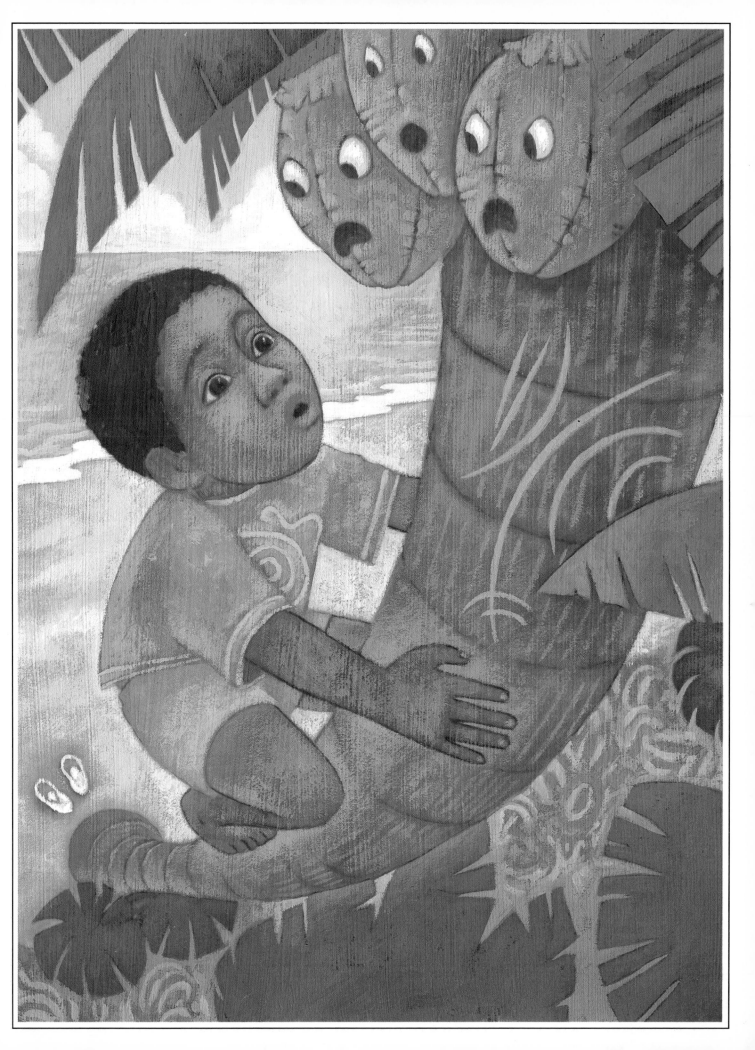

A parrot in the kapok tree called down, *"Muchacho,* don't listen to those coconuts. They're nutty."

"What did you say?" Turo asked.

"What did you say? What did you say?" the parrot repeated. "I don't have to repeat everything someone says. I can say a thing or two on my own. You heard me, *muchacho!"*

"Uh, oh," Turo groaned. "What's going on? Maybe it's just not my day."

"You said it!" snapped his dog.

"What? My dog is talking, too?"

"You heard right. Today's just not your day. Life is rough, rough. I think I'll go and chase the cat."

And then the *cat* spoke. "Can't catch me, you old grouch!"

By now Turo was so hungry and thirsty, he was grouchy himself. "I need a drink," he said, taking up a handful of water from the rain barrel. "At least the rain barrel doesn't talk back."

A frog poked his head out of the water and looked at Turo with big pop eyes. "The rain in this barrel is my property! Next time, *monsieur,* make sure you ask permission before you take a drink."

Turo looked into the rain barrel and scratched his head. "What did that frog say?"

"I said, ask permission before you drink my water. It's okay this time–the first drink is on the house. Next time, remember what I told you, and don't forget to say *s'il vous plaît.*"

The sun was nearly overhead, Turo hadn't even had breakfast, and a bossy frog in the rain barrel was telling him what to do!

"Oh, well, I had my drink. Now I need some food. I'd sure like to *nyam* something tasty and good." Turo took his shovel to the sweet potato patch. "Hello, sweeties, where are you?"

To his surprise the potatoes answered, chanting, *"Ga weg!* Go away! Don't bother us today. *Ga weg!* Go away! This is where we plan to stay."

Turo dropped his shovel. "Talking sweet potatoes? Why is everything talking to me and telling me what to do? This never happened before. What's this *roogoodoo?"*

He ran down the road to his neighbor, Miss Zephyr, to see if she was having the same problem. He saw her talking to a basket full of ripe bananas.

Turo said, "Good morning, Miss Zephyr. When you finish talking to your bananas, could you give me one? I'm so hungry. I had only a handful of water for breakfast. And I practically had to get permission to drink it-from a talking frog in my rain barrel! Everything seems to be talking this morning. The coconuts, the parrot, the dog, the cat, the frog, the sweet potatoes. I wonder why."

"Oh, it's one of those days," said Miss Zephyr. "My bananas have been talking to me all morning, so I'm talking to them, too, to be polite. Here, you can have this one. It hasn't said a word."

But the banana was so small and green and looked so piteously at Turo, he couldn't even eat it.

Turo continued on down the road to the fisherman's house. What was that noise he heard coming from the fish traps?

"Good afternoon, Fisherman," Turo shouted over the hub-bub. "All your fish are talking!"

"What babble-mouths! I guess it's one of those days," said the fisherman. "I haven't sold one. Nobody wants to eat a talking fish."

"I'm hungry, but that's the way I feel about it, too," said Turo. "It's not only the fish. Everything's talking. The coconuts, the parrot, the dog, the cat, the frog, the sweet potatoes, the bananas. I wonder why."

"I don't know," answered the fisherman. "Ask Papa Tata Wanga. He is very knowledgeable. He knows all the island's secrets."

Turo went to the foot of the volcano where Papa Tata Wanga lived. Papa Tata Wanga was sitting in the shade of a mango tree.

"Good evening," Turo greeted Papa Tata Wanga respectfully. "Can I ask you a question? Everything is talking to me today, and I haven't had a bite to eat. The coconuts, the parrot, the dog, the cat, the frog, the sweet potatoes, the bananas, even the fish. They're all talking!"

Papa Tata Wanga looked up at the tree, "Hush, you noisy mangoes! I can hardly hear a word this boy's saying."

Turo talked a little louder. "Can you tell me why everything is talking? My stomach is talking now, too. I'm hungry! Will I ever be able to eat again? Something that doesn't talk back, I mean?"

Papa Tata Wanga shook his finger at the mangoes in the tree. They wouldn't stop chattering, even for a minute.

"I'm sorry you're hungry," Papa Tata Wanga said, "but this is one of those days. It's Palampam Day, the day all things find their voice and say whatever they feel like saying, in any language under the Caribbean sun."

"I never heard of Palampam Day before," Turo said.

"Most people have never heard of Palampam Day. Palampam Day comes only once in a blue moon, when the full moon is truly true blue," said the wise old man. "Here's Papa Tata Wanga's advice: go right home. Turn left. Turn right. Turn all around, and say 'Goodnight.' If the wind's from the east, count three stars, go to bed, and sing:

The moon is blue.

Paladee, paladoo.

Fungee, fish, and kallaloo.

Turo repeated the words:

The moon is blue.

Paladee, paladoo.

Fungee, fish, and kallaloo.

"Magic words work best if you close your eyes," Papa Tata Wanga said. "Then the moon will set. The sun will rise. Palampam Day will be over. Things will go back to the way they were. Parrots will repeat what people say. Dogs will bark the night away. Cats will meow whenever they please. Frogs will croak on hands and knees. Coconuts, sweet potatoes, bananas, fish, and mangoes will be quiet again. Can you remember the words?"

"Oh yes, Papa Tata Wanga. Paladee, paladoo. Thank you! Thank you!"

Turo ran home. He turned left. He turned right. He turned all around and said "Goodnight." The wind was blowing from the east, as it usually did, so he counted three stars and climbed into bed.

Turo closed his eyes and sang:

> *The moon is blue.*
>
> *Paladee, paladoo.*
>
> *Fungee, fish, and kallaloo.*

Papa Tata Wanga was right! The moon set! The sun rose!

In the morning, Turo ate his fill of coconut, sweet potato, banana, fish, and mango. His stomach stopped talking, too.

The island was quiet again, very quiet-so quiet Turo could hear the palm trees whispering in the wind down by Coconut Beach.

AUTHOR'S NOTE

On Palampam Day, what if you could hear all the languages of the West Indies? You'd hear English, French, Dutch, Spanish, and their Creole counterparts, plus Papiamento, which is based on Spanish and spoken in the Dutch West Indies, plus many words with Indian and African roots.

For flavor, the following words appear in this story:

Nyam: eat (from Africa)

Fungee: corn meal mush (from Africa)

Kallaloo: gumbo, a thick, hearty soup (from Africa)

Muchacho: boy (from Spain)

Monsieur: mister (from France)

S'il vous plaît: please (from France)

Ga weg: go away (from Holland)

In the West Indies, *Palampam* and *roogoodoo* imitate the sounds of noise and disorder.

Palampam Day is an imaginary day, though you never know what can happen beneath a tropic sun and moon.